DINOSAURS UNITED

LIGHTNING REX
SPECIES: T. REX
POSITION: STRIKER

COCO
SPECIES: PTEROSAUR
POSITION: MIDFIELDER

ZIGGY
SPECIES: VELOCIRAPTOR
POSITION: MIDFIELDER

SPIKE
SPECIES: TRICERATOPS
POSITION: DEFENDER

DIPPY
SPECIES: DIPLODOCUS
POSITION: GOALIE

Cowardly Custard
PIRATE CREW

CAPTAIN CUSTARD
JOB: BOSS
POSITION: STRIKER

SHIPMATE STUBBLE
JOB: FIRST MATE
POSITION: MIDFIELDER

MUGSY
JOB: COOK
POSITION: MIDFIELDER

SHIPMATE CLAW-DIA
JOB: RIGGER
POSITION: DEFENDER

BARNACLE
JOB: CABIN BOY
POSITION: GOALIE

First published in Great Britain 2017 by Egmont UK Limited,
This edition published 2019 by Dean,
an imprint of Egmont UK Limited,
The Yellow Building, 1 Nicholas Road, London W11 4AN
www.egmont.co.uk

Text copyright © Sam Hay 2017
Illustrations copyright © Daron Parton 2017

Sam Hay and Daron Parton have asserted their moral rights

ISBN 978 0 6035 7761 1
70744/001
Printed in Malaysia

A CIP catalogue record for this title is available from the British Library

DINOSAURS UNITED
and the
Cowardly Custard PIRATE CREW

Sam Hay

Daron Parton

DEAN

Meet

DINOSAURS UNITED –

Spike, Lightning Rex, Dippy, Ziggy and Coco are an awesome five-a-side football team who play in the Fantasy Football League.

They're **fast** and **fun** and always on the ball,

which is just as well because their opponents

use every sneaky trick in the book to

try to **win the cup!**

Dinosaurs United were in a mega muddle.
It was the day of the big football match
against the Cowardly Custard
Pirate Crew and the dinosaurs
couldn't find their kit!

"My boots have vanished!"

"Where's my shirt?"

Lightning Rex called a team meeting.
"If we can't find our kit," he said.
"We can't play the match."

The
dinosaurs
gasped.

They'd never missed
a game before.

Just then something whizzed through the door.
"It's a message in a bottle," Lightning said.
"Let's see what it says . . ."

Yo, ho, ho!
and a bottle of pop,
We've played a trick,
and swiped the lot!
If you want your kit,
then follow this clue.
Yo, ho, ho!
from the
Cowardly Custard
Pirate Crew

Dinosaurs United groaned.
The sneaky pirates had pinched their football stuff!

"Wait!" said Spike. "There's a treasure map on the back of the message."

"Looks like a map of our football pitch," said Dippy, "but what's that big kiss in the corner?"

Lightning laughed. "It's not a kiss. X marks the spot where we'll find our football kit. Come on!"

They raced onto
the pitch . . .

"Ouch!"   "Ooo!"

"Yow!"

But someone
had dumped an
enormous pile
of barnacle
shells there!

"I bet Pirate Barnacle did this!" said Lightning.
"Quick, jump over the shells, like you're
leaping up for a header."

Dinosaurs United made it over the shells.
But they didn't get far . . .

. . . splat!

A large squishy ball burst all over Lightning.

"Water balloons!" he yelled.

Ziggy could see
who was firing at them.

"It's Shipmate Stubble!" she shouted.
"Hit the balloons back at him, like you're saving a goal!"

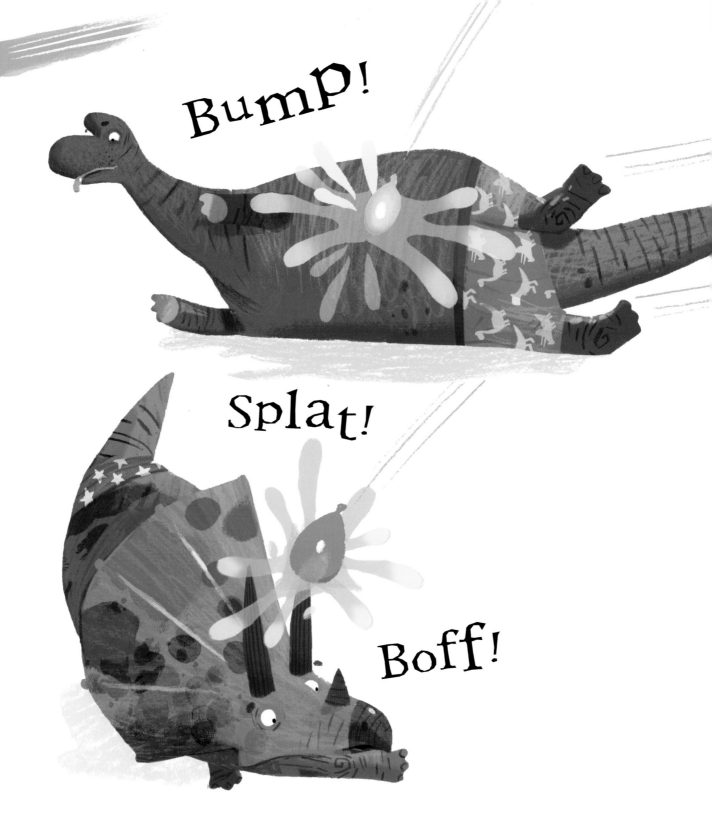

The dinosaurs made it past the cannon, but the pirates had more tricks up their salty sleeves . . .

Shipmate Claw-dia dashed past with
a sneaky grin on her face.

"Watch out!" Lightning yelled.

"Crabs!"

An army of nippy crabs was marching towards them.

"Ouch!"

Ziggy cried.

"One's got me."

"Hold on . . ." called Coco, and she lifted Ziggy up, while the rest of the dinosaurs dodged round the crabs.

"It's like dribbling in a match,"
Spike puffed. "But it's nearly time for
kick-off. We've got to find our kit!"

The dinosaurs **zoomed** down the pitch. But when they got to the end there was no sign of their kit.

Lightning scratched his scaly chin. "I don't understand it. All I can see is the half-time snack trolley."

Dippy's tummy rumbled, "Custard doughnuts. Mmm!" He dived for the plate. But as he jumped, he bumped into the trolley and knocked it over . . .

"Whoah! Dippy,
you brain-o-saurus!"
Lightning shouted. "You found
our kit!"

Just then the referee blew his whistle.

peeeeeeeep!

The match was about to start!

As the dinosaurs ran onto the pitch, Captain Custard couldn't believe his eyes. "Shiver me timbers!" he gasped. "You found your stuff!"

"And now we're ready to play football," Lightning said.

"F-f-football?" Captain Custard said,
his knees knocking,
his cutlass shaking.

"W-w-w-we **never** play football.
W-w-w-we only like to play tricks on people!"

And with that, the Cowardly Custard Crew legged it back to their ship.

"AwWW," Ziggy groaned. "I was looking forward to chasing those sea dogs round the pitch."

"Never mind," said Coco.
"We've already played a bit of football."

It was true. Dinosaurs United had done
some great headers and saved
loads of water balloon goals.
Not to mention dribbling
past lots of nippy crabs.

Lightning chuckled. "And we've got some pirate treasure –

Custard doughnuts
for everyone!

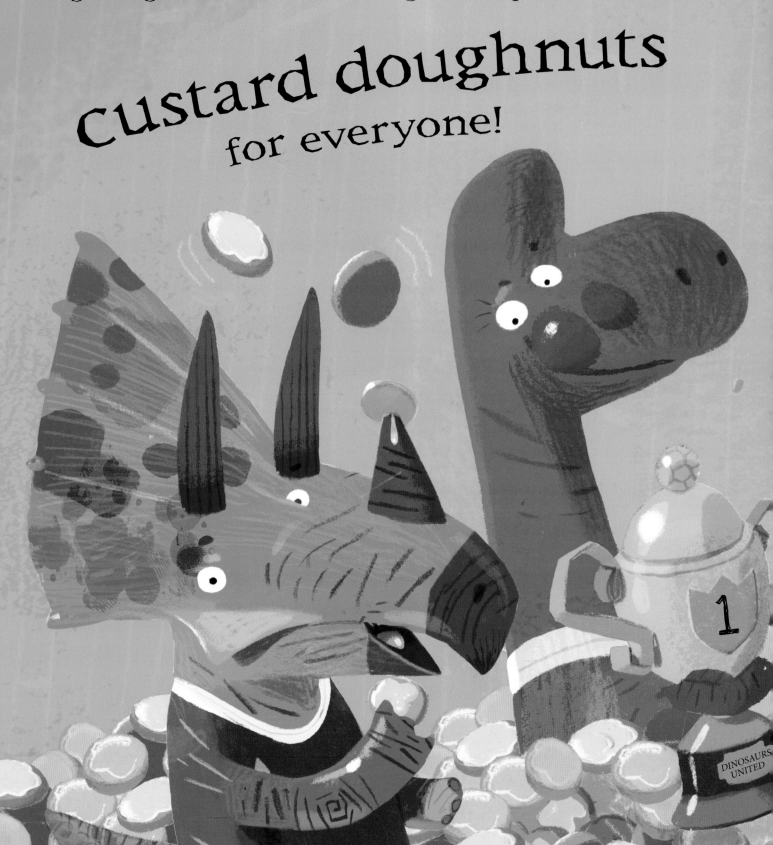

Hooray for **DINOSAURS UNITED!**"